The Everyday Train

The Everyday Train

by Amy Ehrlich · Pictures by Martha Alexander

THE DIAL PRESS · NEW YORK

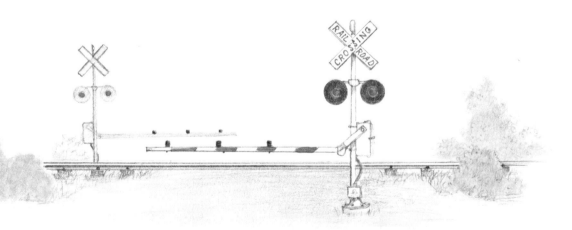

Text copyright © 1977 by Amy Ehrlich
Pictures copyright © 1977 by Martha Alexander
All rights reserved
First Printing
Separations by Rainbows Inc.
Printed in the United States of America
by Holyoke Lithograph Co. Inc.
Bound by Economy Bookbinding Corp.

Library of Congress Cataloging in Publication Data

Ehrlich, Amy, 1942-
The everyday train.

Summary: A little girl loves to watch the
freight train pass her house every day.
[1. Railroads—Trains—Fiction]
I. Alexander, Martha G.   II. Title.
PZ7.E328Ev   [E]
ISBN 0-8037-2191-9   76-42922
ISBN 0-8037-2192-7 lib. bdg.

for my sister, Jane

Outside Jane's house

there was a train track and a train that went by every day. Jane
loved the train.

She waited for it in the morning, she remembered it in the after-
noon, and at night she rode it in her dreams.

The train did not really carry people. It was a freight train.

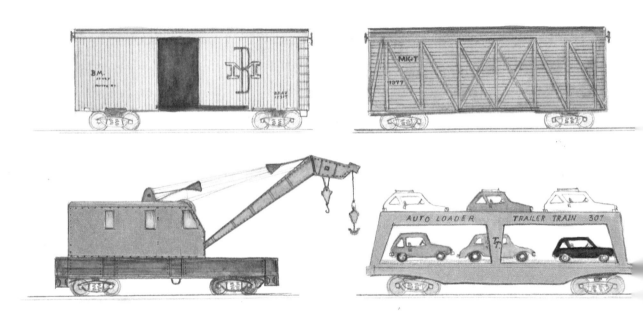

Boxcars, flatcars,

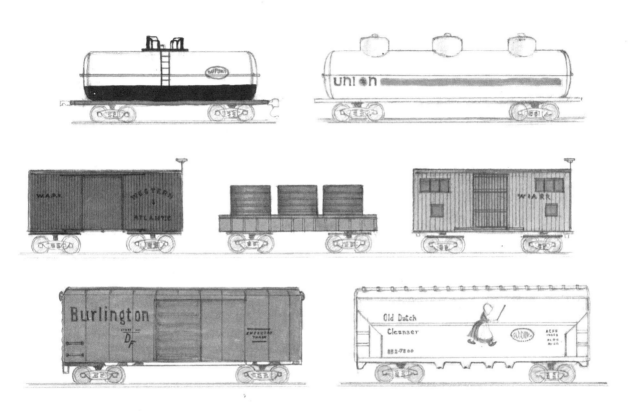

fuel cars, old cars, new cars, many cars, few cars.

Every day the train looked different. But the sound of the whistle
way off in the distance never changed. Whenever she heard it,
Jane knew that the train was coming through.

The sound of the whistle told Jane to get ready.

If she was reading a book, she stopped in the middle.

If she was climbing up a tree,
she climbed down.

If she was helping her mother bake cookies, she grabbed one and ran outside. The train was coming through.

The path to the track zigzagged among pine trees and ended in
a grassy place.

Jane stood waiting. The air around her hummed with the rocking of the cars and the clacking of the wheels. Rocking, clacking, rocking, clacking. Jane jammed her fingers in her ears and felt the ground shake under her feet. Here it came. The train.

Whoosh. The engine went past, bright red and fast. Through a window up in front, Jane could see the engineer. Every day she waved.

The engineer was busy driving, blowing the whistle at crossings, watching for cows on the track. But every day when Jane waved, the engineer waved back.

The engine pulled the train. Cars and cars and cars of it. One, two, three flatcars. Four, five fuel cars. Six, seven, eight, nine, ten, eleven boxcars.

The boxcars kept coming. Erie Lackawanna and Rock Island.
Canadian Pacific and Topeka. Circle O and Santa Fe.

The names got blurry. The train's wind stung Jane's eyes and made tears run down her face. All she could see now was a long, snaky line of changing colors.

Where had the train come from? Where did the train go? Jane
closed her eyes.

She saw a long, long silvery track going through farmland where horses grazed, past cities, over rivers and high mountains. Here and there along the track people were waiting to wave to the train. Was one of them a girl like her? Jane wondered.

When she opened her eyes, the train was passing slower. It was time to play What-Color-Is-the-Caboose-Today. This was a game Jane had made up.

Whether she won or lost depended on the color of the caboose.
If it was green, she lost. If it was red, she won.

Today the caboose was red, and Jane was a winner.

She watched the train get smaller and smaller going away into the distance.

Then it swung around a curve and was gone. The empty track shone in the sunlight.

It was exactly twelve noon when Jane ran home to tell her mother all about the train.